It's Christmas, David!

By

David Shannon

THE BLUE SKY PRESS

An Imprint of Scholastic Inc. • New York

To my family, with love.

THE BLUE SKY PRESS

Copyright © 2010 by David Shannon

All rights reserved.

No part of this publication may be reproduced, stored in a retrieval system, or

transmitted in any form or by any means, electronic, mechanical, photocopying,

recording, or otherwise, without written permission of the publisher.

For information regarding permission, please write to: Permissions Department,

Scholastic Inc., 557 Broadway, New York, New York 10012.

SCHOLASTIC, THE BLUE SKY PRESS, and associated logos are trademarks

and/or registered trademarks of Scholastic Inc.

Library of Congress catalog card number: 2009046529

ISBN 978-0-545-14311-0

10 9 8 7 6 5 4 3 2 1   10 11 12 13 14

Printed in Singapore   46

First printing, September 2010

At Christmastime,
everyone always said . . .

DA

Naughty list, naughty

Santa's going to bring you a lump of coal!

Don't start yet! Seat your grandmother.
No yawning at the dinner table.
That's the wrong fork!

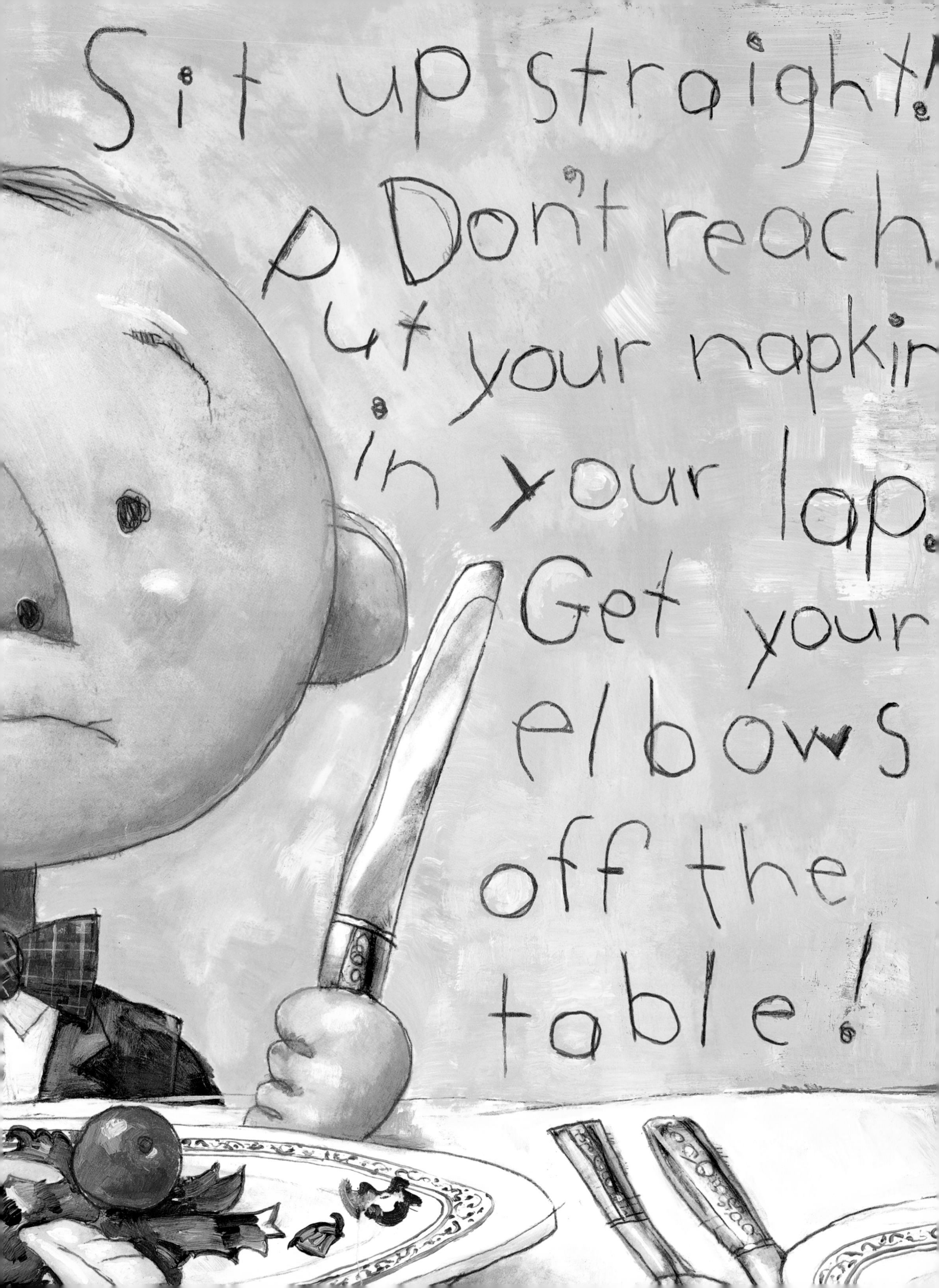
Sit up straight!
Don't reach
Put your napkin
in your lap.
Get your
elbows
off the
table!

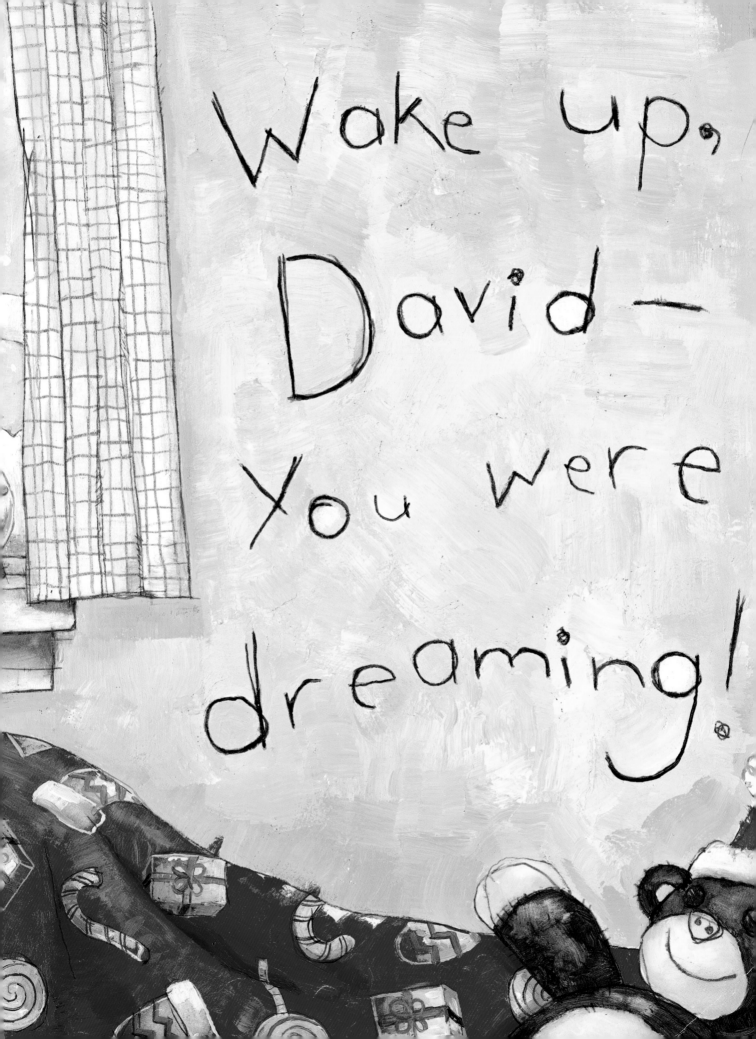